Drusilla
and Her Brothers

DYAN SHELDON

ILLUSTRATED BY
EMMA DODSON

WALKER
BOOKS

For Esther and her brother
D.S.

For Amira and her brothers
E.D.

This is a work of fiction. Names, characters, places and incidents
either are the product of the author's imagination or, if real, are used
fictitiously. All statements, activities, stunts, descriptions, information
and material of any other kind contained herein are included for
entertainment purposes only and should not be relied on for
accuracy or replicated as they may result in injury.

First published 2009 by Walker Books Ltd
87 Vauxhall Walk, London SE11 5HJ

2 4 6 8 10 9 7 5 3

Text © 2009 Dyan Sheldon
Illustrations © 2009 Emma Dodson

The right of Dyan Sheldon and Emma Dodson to be identified as author
and illustrator respectively of this work has been asserted by them in
accordance with the Copyright, Designs and Patents Act 1988

This book has been typeset in Bembo Educational
and Randumhouse

Printed and bound in China

All rights reserved. No part of this book may be reproduced, transmitted
or stored in an information retrieval system in any form or by any means,
graphic, electronic or mechanical, including photocopying, taping and
recording, without prior written permission from the publisher.

British Library Cataloguing in Publication Data:
a catalogue record for this book is available from the British Library

ISBN: 978-1-4063-1609-4

www.walker.co.uk

Drusilla's Brothers Are Bored

Drusilla was a quiet, thoughtful
little girl. She had a small toy
hippopotamus and four big brothers.

Drusilla's brothers were Harlan,
Kal, CJ and Joe.

The hippopotamus's name was
Mrs Mu.

Mrs Mu went everywhere with Drusilla.

Harlan, Kal, CJ and Joe went nowhere with her.

"You're too little to hang out with us," declared Harlan.

Kal nodded. "You only get in the way."

"You're a baby," said CJ.

"I'm not a baby," argued Drusilla. "I'm just short."

"A short baby," said Joe.

9

Drusilla's brothers wouldn't let her join their games.

They left her at home when they went off on their bikes.

They wouldn't even take her to the park with them so she could fly her kite while they played football.

10

There was only one thing Drusilla's
brothers liked to do with her,
and that was tease her.
They moved her things
around. They filled her
pockets with stones.
They stuffed her
backpack with
empty packets. They nicked
chips from her plate when
she wasn't
looking.
They were
always thinking
of new and better
ways to annoy her.

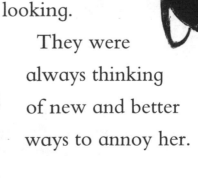

11

But, being a quiet, thoughtful little girl, Drusilla wasn't very easy to upset.

No matter what her brothers did, she never cried, or shouted, or threw a tantrum as other little girls might have done.

Drusilla had learned to ignore them.

Mrs Mu, of course, was calm itself.

"This is boring," said Kal.

"Too right," said CJ.

"It's no fun teasing someone who never gets annoyed," said Joe.

"There has to be *something* we can do to get a rise out of her," said Harlan.

One morning
Drusilla was getting
dressed, when she
discovered that her new
pink shoes weren't where she'd left
them the night before.

"My brothers must be playing one
of their tricks," she told Mrs Mu. She
could hear the boys whispering out on
the landing.

As always, Mrs Mu simply smiled.

"You're right," said Drusilla. "It's
not the end of the world." And she
went to her wardrobe
and got out her old
trainers instead.

14

"She's not meant
to do that," Kal complained.
"She's meant to go mad," grumbled CJ.
"Or cry," added Joe.
"We'll have to try something
else," said Harlan.

15

That afternoon Drusilla and
Mrs Mu were sitting in the
garden reading a book.

They had just reached the best bit,
when the sprinkler suddenly burst into
action, soaking them both.

Drusilla and Mrs Mu jumped
out of their deckchair.

Drusilla could
hear her brothers
laughing
back by the
house. "It's
them again," she
whispered to Mrs Mu.
Mrs Mu just smiled.

"You're right," said Drusilla.
"It's only water."

And she moved
the chair to where the
sprinkler couldn't
reach it. She and
Mrs Mu would dry in
no time in the sun.

18

"Why isn't she upset?" Joe whined.

"Yeah, why can't she act like everybody else's little sisters?" moaned Kal and CJ.

"There has to be *something* that will really bother her," said Harlan. "We just have to work out what it is."

That night Drusilla
was taking a bath
and Mrs Mu was
floating beside her in
the inflatable soap
dish, when the light
went out.

"That'll be
the boys again,"
sighed Drusilla.
She could hear her
brothers shuffling
restlessly outside the
bathroom door.

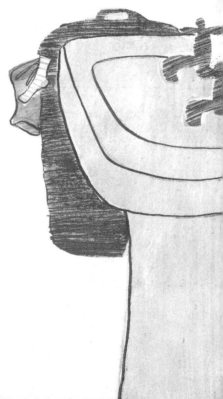

But even in the dark Drusilla could
see Mrs Mu's smile.

"You were right," said Drusilla.
"One should always be prepared."
And she took her torch from the
shelf behind her and switched it on.

"Why isn't she scared?"
hissed Joe.

"She really is *too* much,"
muttered CJ.

"She's no fun at all," said Kal.

23

But Harlan, who was the
eldest and the cleverest, said,
"Don't worry. This time
I've got a brilliant idea."

Where Is Mrs Mu?

The next morning Drusilla woke
up with a start. Mrs Mu wasn't lying
beside her as usual.

She looked under the duvet, the
pillows and the bed, but Mrs Mu was
nowhere to be seen.

This was the worst
trick her brothers
had ever played, but
Drusilla managed not
to scream or cry.

She marched across
the landing to their
bedroom.

Her
brothers
were
all still
in their
pyjamas.

Harlan smiled down from the top bunk. "What do you want?"

"I want Mrs Mu," said Drusilla.

Kal smiled up from the bunk under Harlan's. "So what?"

"You lot took her, that's what." Drusilla held out her hand. "Now give her back."

"We don't have your stupid hippo," laughed CJ.

Joe fiddled with his shoelace. "Yeah, we wouldn't want *that*. It's a baby's toy."

Their mother appeared in the doorway. "What's going on in here?"

Drusilla pointed at her brothers. "They've taken Mrs Mu."

Their mother frowned. "Oh, boys!"

"It's not true," protested Kal. "We haven't touched her."

CJ looked hurt. "Cross my heart, Mum."

Joe was still fiddling with his shoelace. "Drusilla's probably left her somewhere," he mumbled. "She'll turn up."

"You can search our room if you want," offered Harlan. "We have nothing to hide."

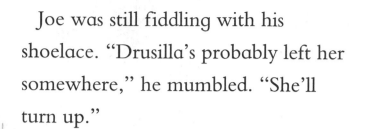

Drusilla and her
mother searched the
boys' bedroom. But
although they found a ball
of gardening twine in one of the desks
and a heap of Lego pieces
under a bed, there was
no sign of Mrs Mu.

"It looks like your
brothers are telling the
truth this time." Drusilla's mother put
the ball of twine in her pocket to return
it to the shed. "You must have left her
somewhere and forgotten."

"But I had her last night when I fell
asleep," insisted Drusilla.

Their mother turned to the boys with a sigh. "If I find out that you have taken Mrs Mu, there'll be no more football in the park for the rest of the year. Is that understood?"

Kal, CJ and Joe nodded.

"Don't worry," said Harlan. "You won't."

After breakfast Drusilla looked in
the places where her brothers usually
hid her things.

"Mrs Mu!" she
called as she hunted
in the living room.
"Mrs Mu, where are
you?"

She emerged from
the fireplace covered
in soot.

Harlan looked up from
the book he was reading by
the window. "Gosh," he said.
"I wonder where she could be."

"Mrs Mu!" called Drusilla as she rummaged through the kitchen. "Where are you, Mrs Mu?"

She had to shake the ice off her fingers when she'd finished searching the freezer.

36

Kal was putting away some carrier bags. "It's too bad you can't remember where you left her." He shook his head sadly. "At this rate, you may never get her back."

"Mrs Mu!" Drusilla shouted
as she poked around the bathroom.
"Mrs Mu, where are you?"

She found her new pink shoes
in the linen cupboard, but no small
hippopotamus.

"Still no luck?" CJ threw a towel
into the laundry basket. "Oh dear,
I hope she's not gone
for good."

Drusilla stomped
across the lawn, calling,
"Mrs Mu! Mrs Mu!"
When she came out of the shed she
was covered in cobwebs,
but there was no smiling
hippo in her hands.

Joe was sitting by the pond.
"Are you going to start crying
now?" he asked.

Drusilla went up to her room straight after supper.

Harlan, Kal, CJ and Joe followed her up the stairs, calling, "Mrs Mu! Mrs Mu! Oh, where can you be?"

"You'd better give her back," warned Drusilla.

Harlan shrugged.
"But we don't have her."
Kal nodded. "That's right."
"You've looked everywhere,"
said CJ. "She isn't here."
"She *has* to be,"
insisted Drusilla
stubbornly.
"Not like
you'll ever
find her,"
muttered Joe.

"Don't be so sure of that,"

said Drusilla.

Drusilla Gets Her Own Back

When Drusilla got into bed that
night she kept her light on for a while.

She was thinking.

Her brothers hadn't gone anywhere
all day, so Mrs Mu had to be somewhere
around the house.

But *where*? She took the photograph of
her and Mrs Mu from the bedside table.

"I wish you
could tell
me where
you are,
Mrs Mu,"
Drusilla
whispered.

Mrs Mu smiled
back at her the way
she always did.

"You're right,"
said Drusilla. "I'm
not thinking
hard enough."

Her brothers must have left some clues. Something she hadn't noticed at the time.

She closed her eyes and went back over the day in her mind.

She saw herself in her brothers' room.

Harlan, Kal and CJ were all smiling. There was nothing unusual about that. Joe was fiddling with his shoelace.

Drusilla opened her eyes. *Shoes!* Her brothers were in their pyjamas, but they were wearing shoes! They must have been outside.

50

"But I looked in the garden,"
she sighed.

Mrs Mu continued to smile from
the photograph. *Think … think …*

think…

she seemed
to say.

Drusilla
thought.

She pictured her brothers' room.

She saw the usual piles of clothes and games.

She saw the ball of twine in Kal's desk and the Lego pieces under the bed.

What was Kal doing with the garden string? Where was the large plastic jar the boys kept the Lego in?

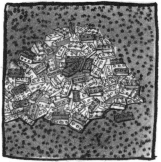

52

She opened
her eyes again.
"It just
doesn't make
any sense,"
Drusilla
informed
the photo
of her and Mrs Mu.
"They can't have posted you
somewhere. They never went out."

Mrs Mu smiled.
Think … think …
think…

Shoes … twine … missing jar… Drusilla squeezed her eyes shut very tightly.

She saw Harlan sitting by the garden window … Kal with carrier bags in the kitchen … CJ putting a wet towel in the basket … Joe sitting by the pond.

54

"That's it!" cried Drusilla. She kissed the photo, snuggled under the covers and went to sleep.

The next morning Drusilla was up very early. She went straight to the pond.

Pinned under a large rock, she found the end of a long piece of green twine that dangled into the water.

She tugged slowly on the twine.

Centimetre by centimetre, the large plastic jar her brothers used for their Lego rose from the pond.

Drusilla opened the jar and pulled out the carrier bags stuffed inside.

From out of the bags she took a small hippo. Mrs Mu was a bit damp, but she was still smiling.

Drusilla hugged her tight. "Oh, Mrs Mu, I'm so glad to see you."

Mrs Mu was glad to see her too.

After breakfast Harlan, Kal, CJ and
Joe all got ready to go to the park.

But when they came downstairs with
their football, Drusilla was waiting by
the door for them with her kite.

"Where do you think
you're going?" asked Harlan.

Drusilla turned so
they could see the small
hippopotamus peeking
out of her backpack.

"With you. You're going to help me and Mrs Mu fly our kite."

The boys all laughed. "Why would we do that?" asked Harlan.

Drusilla opened her mouth, but before she could answer, their mother came down the hall.

"You've found Mrs Mu!" she cried. "Where was she?"

Drusilla looked at Harlan.

Harlan looked at his brothers, and then he grabbed Drusilla's hand. "We don't have time now, Mum. We're taking Drusilla to the park with us to fly her kite."

"Why, isn't that nice," said their mother. "You have fun!"

"Oh, we will!" said Drusilla.

And she and Mrs Mu smiled.